Jo Weston's Netball Besties

PENGUIN BOOKS

UK | USA | Canada | Ireland | Australia
India | New Zealand | South Africa | China

Penguin Random House Australia

Penguin Random House Australia is part of the Penguin Random House group of companies whose addresses can be found at global.penguinrandomhouse.com.

First published by Penguin Books, an imprint of Penguin Random House Australia Pty Ltd, in 2026

Cover design by Julie Hally
Internal design by Caroline Lee © Penguin Random House Australia 2026
Cover and internal illustrations by Sam Loman
Author photograph © Grant Treeby

Printed and bound in Australia by Griffin Press, an accredited ISO AS/NZS 14001 Environmental Management Systems printer

NATIONAL LIBRARY OF AUSTRALIA

A catalogue record for this book is available from the National Library of Australia

FSC www.fsc.org MIX Paper | Supporting responsible forestry FSC® C018684

ISBN 978 1 76 134856 3 (Paperback)

Penguin Random House Australia uses papers that are natural and recyclable products, made from wood grown in sustainable forests. The logging and manufacture processes are expected to conform to the environmental regulations of the country of origin.

We at Penguin Random House Australia acknowledge that Aboriginal and Torres Strait Islander peoples are the Traditional Custodians and the first storytellers of the lands on which we live and work. We honour Aboriginal and Torres Strait Islander peoples' continuous connection to Country, waters, skies and communities. We celebrate Aboriginal and Torres Strait Islander stories, traditions and living cultures; and we pay our respects to Elders past and present.

Jo Weston's Netball Besties

The Disappearing Trophy

Written by Jess Black
Illustrated by Sam Loman

PENGUIN BOOKS

CHAPTER ONE

'Oh no! I'm soooo late!'

Jo ***bounces*** on her feet as she fills up her water bottle. The clock above the kitchen sink blinks 7.45am – the exact time the school bus usually appears at the end of the long gravel driveway that leads up to the Weston farmhouse.

As the bottle takes *forever* to fill, she glances at a framed photo nearby on the kitchen bench. It's an action shot of Jo and Ava on the court – taken at half-time during the professional netball game they got to attend in the city in the school holidays. They'd had the most ***amazing*** time, playing netball and solving another mystery. The energy of the photo perfectly captures how she felt in the moment. Completely ***electric!***

'You better get moving, Jo!' her mum calls from the bedroom.

Jo screws the lid on her bottle and crams it into her school bag. 'I'm going!' she calls and bolts for the door. Her dog Billie is hot on her heels.

Jo slings her school bag over one shoulder and pauses in the doorway. 'Remember,' she calls out, 'it's Monday, so I finish late today – we've got training!'

'I'm picking you up!' her dad shouts from the hallway, just as the screen door slams shut behind her.

Jo ***bounds*** down the front steps, shoes crunching on gravel. To her left, a few cows graze peacefully in the morning light. Jo notices that her favourite, Moo-dini, is present and accounted for. Moo-dini has a habit of escaping, so Jo is relieved to see that her errant cow is where she should be.

To her right, rows of walnut trees stretch into the mist – tall and still, with their branches bare except for tight buds. Living at Talma Valley Nut Farm means Jo is surrounded by chestnut, hazelnut and walnut trees, plus an endless supply of fresh air and early-morning activity. The earthy smell of damp soil mixes with the frost still clinging to the grass.

Her breath forms little puffs in the cold air as she picks up speed. Billie, the Westons' ***always-energetic*** Australian Shepherd, races ahead, her fluffy tail flying behind her.

'You're cheating!' Jo pants, running hard. 'You don't have a school bag dragging you down – and also, four legs? Not fair, Billie.'

Billie yaps ***gleefully*** and bounds to the front gate, waiting with her tail wagging and eyes trained on the road. Her whole body is vibrating with excitement.

Just as Jo begins to panic that she's missed the bus, she hears the familiar engine rumble from around the bend. Relief floods through her and she puts on a final burst of speed.

The old yellow bus pulls into view and slows to a stop. Jock, the driver, is a fixture of her mornings, always

wearing the same cap pulled low over his brow. The bus's patterned fabric seats have long since faded, but they smell faintly of eucalyptus and pencil shavings – comforting in a familiar way.

'Bye, Billie!' Jo says, giving Billie a final pat. Billie's legs tremble with

anticipation. Her favourite part of the day is about to begin – racing the bus.

Jo slips through the gate and latches it, then clambers up the bus steps, puffing.

'Sorry!'

'Morning, Jo,' Jock says, raising his hand for their daily fist bump.

'Thanks for waiting,' Jo adds as they connect hands. 'I can*not* be late today!'

'Of course!' Jock grins. 'Interschool netball comp on Friday.'

'It's our last training session,' Jo adds as she makes her way towards her usual seat.

'Go Talma Valley!' calls Jock.

Jock shifts into gear and the bus groans forward. Jo walks the aisle, waving at familiar faces, then slides into her usual seat by the window. The seat next to her is empty – but not for long.

Outside, Billie sprints beside the moving bus with ***wild joy***, tongue flopping and paws flying. As usual, she wins the race. She skids to a halt at the fence line, gives one last bark, then bounds back towards home, tail spinning like a propeller.

Jo's best friend, Ava, is waiting at the next stop. She moved to Talma Valley when her family bought the sheep farm next door to the Westons not long ago and the girls now do everything together – including netball. She boards with her usual easy hop, giving Jock a cheerful grin before plonking into the seat beside Jo.

'Hi,' Ava says, eyeing Jo's school bag. 'Got your kit?'

Jo taps the top of her bag. 'Packed last night. Now remind me how much I've told you about last year's final?'

Ava ***groans***, already laughing. 'If you say one more word about Talma Valley Public School being the reigning champions, I will pass out from pressure.'

Jo grins. 'You need to understand the history of the game, Ava.'

Ava glances at her watch. 'Reckon we can squeeze in a bit of practice before school?'

'Absolutely,' says Jo. 'And we've got enough bus time for me to give you a recap of the *entire* final,' she teases.

'Aaaah!' Ava **slumps** down in her seat. 'You're impossible.'

'Picture it,' Jo begins, slipping into storyteller mode. 'It was a fresh morning in Talma Valley when long-time rivals Talma Valley Public and East Ridge Public School came head to head in what would come to be known as a legendary game . . .'

Ava groans again and sinks deeper into her seat.

CHAPTER TWO

Ava and Jo arrive at school with time to spare before the day officially begins. After hopping off the bus, they dodge a stray football on the oval and jog up towards the netball courts, eager to squeeze in a warm-up.

But Cassandra and Amaya have already claimed the space.

Both girls are in class with Jo and Ava, and they also happen to be ***excellent*** netball players. They'll be a big part of the final. The sound of netball drills cuts through the chilly air – crisp catches, sharp passes and mutters of frustration at missed shots. Frost still lingers in the shaded corners of the asphalt, melting slowly under the brightening sun.

'Busy morning,' Jo murmurs as they see that the basketball court is also full. 'The boys' team are defending champions too and they've got their finals game the week after ours. So, it's all happening!'

Cassandra and Amaya are locked into a tight passing rhythm, moving with precision. Cassandra's footwork is clean, her arms slicing through the air as she pivots. Amaya moves like liquid, light on her feet, each step smooth and quiet. They don't play club netball – but they should.

'Lucky for us they're on our team,' Jo says, watching with ***admiration***.

'I don't understand why they don't play club,' Ava murmurs. 'They'd crush it.'

'I think they're both pretty busy. Amaya does gymnastics all year and Cassandra . . . I'm not sure. Maybe she doesn't like our team name – the Junior Wildcats?'

'Who doesn't like cats?' Ava frowns.

'Heaps of people,' Jo replies with a laugh. 'Especially nut farmers – cats are hopeless with possums.'

Tamsin and Jane arrive together, full of ***bounce*** and ***banter***.

'Last training session tonight!' Jane beams, bouncing her netball. 'I'm so pumped for Friday.'

'I'm nervous,' says Tamsin, stretching her arms. 'What if we just got lucky last year?'

'Luck had nothing to do with it,' says Jane firmly.

Jo waves to Cassandra and Amaya. 'Mind if we jump in?'

'For sure,' Cassandra calls, not breaking stride.

The six girls quickly fall into a passing drill. Ava to Jane, Jane to Tamsin, Tamsin to Amaya, Amaya to Cassandra, then Cassandra to Jo.

Cassandra whips the ball to Jo – fast and clean.

Jo catches it with a wince. 'Someone ate their Weet-Bix this morning.'

'Too much?' Cassandra asks, raising an eyebrow.

'I can take it,' Jo replies. 'I need to keep up. I'm on a ***winning team!***'

'Come on, let's keep moving!' Jane claps her hands.

They shift into structured drills: shoulder passes, quick dodges, strong holds. It's fast-paced and focused – more like finals prep than a casual warm-up.

Then, suddenly, a ***rogue*** basketball bounces across the netball court.

'Watch out, Ava!' Jo calls.

Ava ducks just in time. Cassandra snatches the ball midair with a clean grab.

They turn to see Max, captain of the boys' basketball team, jogging towards them. He raises a hand in apology.

'Oops – sorry!'

'You could've hurt Ava!' Cassandra snaps, the edge in her voice sharp.

'I'm really sorry, it was a bad pass,'

Max says, offering a tentative smile. 'Lucky you caught it, though.'

Cassandra returns the ball with a pass that looks more like a serve. 'Stick to your own court.'

Max catches it and hesitates, his face unreadable. But Cassandra has already turned away.

Jo notices something shift – the atmosphere is more ***charged*** than before. Sure, there's always been a bit of banter between the netballers and basketballers, but this . . . feels different.

'One more set!' Cassandra calls, rallying the girls.

They finish the drill, though something lingers in the air.

As the bell rings, Jo collects her bag, cheeks flushed, heart still ***thumping***.

'We'll make it ours again this year,' she whispers.

'You promised – no pressure until lunch,' Ava warns.

'Fine,' Jo smirks. 'Have I filled you in on the netball-versus-basketball rivalry we have here? It's a pretty funny story . . .'

'You're truly nuts,' Ava sighs.

'I live on a nut farm. What did you expect?' Jo grins.

CHAPTER THREE

Jo and Ava burst through the school corridor, puffing, bags thumping against their backs. The corridor hums with morning noise – locker doors slamming and weekend news exchanged. They almost ***collide*** headfirst with the new work-experience person, Alannah, but she steps aside to let them pass just in time.

'Sorry'! Jo says breathlessly.

'It's all good,' Alannah replies cheerfully.

Jo tugs at Ava's sleeve.

'There she is,' says Jo, smiling.

Beside the row of lockers is a glass cabinet packed with awards and plaques. The cabinet **gleams** under the hallway lights. Dust has been carefully wiped away, each item perfectly aligned. But on the top row, in all its glory, sits the netball trophy. The nameplate proudly displays: *Talma Valley Public School – District Netball Champions.*

'You little beauty,' Jo whispers.

'I swear you check in on this trophy every day,' Ava says.

'Just saying hello,' Jo replies, placing her hand on the glass. 'I want her to know she's appreciated.' The smooth, cold surface of the glass catches her breath for a moment, fogging faintly.

'Now you're being a weirdo,' Ava teases. 'It's not going to sprout wings and fly away.'

'You never know,' laughs Jo. 'stranger things have happened.'

The sharp call of a teacher snaps their attention back to the present.

'Assembly now, girls!'

Students file past, the current carrying Jo and Ava along with it. They take their usual spots near the back of the gym, ***squeezed*** in with the rest of Year Six. The air smells faintly of disinfectant and wooden floor polish, with a hint of something stale and musty coming from the Lost And Found bucket near the back corner.

Rows of students ***shuffle*** and ***murmur*** as they settle.

After the Acknowledgement of Country and school anthem, the school kids once again take their seats on the floor.

At the front of the room, Mr Redfern, the principal, waits at the podium. He's tall and broad-shouldered, in a grey sports coat over a black crew neck T-shirt. Lately he's taken to wearing streetwear trainers with skinny jeans and nobody really knows what to think about this.

'Good morning, everyone,' Mr Redfern begins before launching into a long list of announcements:

book parade dates, uniform infractions and weekend sports successes. His voice rises and falls with practised rhythm – calm, orderly, a little too slow for Jo's current heart rate.

Jo lets her mind wander. She replays the morning at the court – Cassandra's OTT reaction to Max, the way the ball ***zipped*** through drills like they were already in a final.

Finally, Mr Redfern clears his throat and smiles. 'To finish, I want to give a big shoutout to our senior netball team – reigning district champions and once again finalists this Friday!'

Applause breaks out. Jo and Ava grin.

'Can the team please stand up?' Mr Redfern adds.

How embarrassing! thinks Jo, but she stands and looks around at the rest of the team. There's Ava, of course, and Kiki, Rose, Tamsin, Jane, Amaya, Holly, Imogen . . . but no Cassandra.

That's weird, thinks Jo. *Where is she?*

The entire hall ***applauds*** the team. Then, just as it looks as if they can sit down again, Mr Redfern motions to Mrs Jensen.

'Can we grab the trophy?' he asks her.

She nods and steps offstage, heels clicking briskly against the varnished gym floor.

He continues. 'It's great to recognise sporting ***excellence***. Last year the team showed pride, teamwork and real resilience, and we are all behind them this year as they fight to retain the title.'

Mrs Jensen returns empty-handed. She leans in and whispers something to Mr Redfern.

Mr Redfern pauses. There's a slight wrinkle between his eyebrows before he straightens again. 'Seems the trophy isn't in its usual spot. Probably being cleaned. Nothing to worry about!'

More applause. But Jo's brain is spinning.

They just saw the trophy a few minutes ago.

She scans the room again. Cassandra is definitely not at assembly – but neither is Max.

Jo's intuition tells her that something is not quite right.

CHAPTER FOUR

'***Psst!*** This way.' As they file out of assembly, Jo nudges Ava to take the exit that leads back to the trophy cabinet. It's in the opposite direction to their Year Six classroom, but Jo doesn't care. She's too busy wondering how a trophy they saw minutes ago could have suddenly vanished.

Jo and Ava are first out of the hall and run towards the cabinet. Jo can tell immediately that something is different. She feels her heart ***thud*** in her chest.

Mrs Jensen was right. The trophy has gone! The cabinet looks colder, lonelier somehow, like it has never held anything important at all.

The rest of the netball team – including Jane, Tamsin, Kiki and Rose – along with a few curious bystanders gather around. A low murmur ripples through the group.

'Where's the trophy?' asks Jane, her voice tight with confusion.

'Do you really think it's been taken for cleaning?' Kiki frowns, pressing a palm to the glass like she might feel an answer.

'Where else would it be?' Rose chimes in, looking between Jo and Ava as if they might know.

'Maybe it's been stolen . . .' someone mutters.

'Who would want to steal a trophy?' says another.

'As a prank,' offers someone else.

'No, it's *gone* gone.'

The words hang in the air – not ***dramatic***, but final.

'We don't know that,' says Jo firmly.

Behind them, the buzz of conversation continues. Near the lockers, a group of Year Six girls cluster together. One of them leans in and whispers something just loud enough to catch.

'I saw Max near the trophy cabinet before the bell rang. Like, *right* before assembly started. He was just standing there.'

A few heads turn.

'You sure?' someone asks, eyebrows raised.

The girl shrugs, her voice still hushed but certain. 'I mean . . . yeah.'

Jo's brain clicks into gear, but before she can open her mouth, Cassandra appears – suddenly, like she's materialised from nowhere. Her cheeks are flushed, hair slightly wind-blown, like she's been running.

Jo frowns. *Where did you come from?*

'I heard that too,' Cassandra says quickly. 'Max was totally ***lurking*** this morning.'

Jo's head snaps around. 'Hang on. Ava and I were right beside the trophy just before assembly and Max wasn't here and he wasn't *lurking*,' she says firmly.

Everyone turns to look at her.

Cassandra shrugs, lifting her chin slightly. 'I can only tell you what I saw.'

Cassandra's tone is firm. To Jo's dismay, she sees other kids nodding. Jo can tell that lots of the kids believe Cassandra; they're pulling ***shocked*** expressions.

'Let's take this one step at a time,' Jo says. Her voice is steady but urgent. 'Nobody knows for sure what happened.'

'Exactly,' Ava adds. 'It's not like it's disappeared into thin air.'

Cassandra folds her arms. 'Well, I think it's weird. And I don't see Max rushing in to explain himself.'

'He's probably gone to class,' Amaya points out from behind them, her voice calm and even.

Jo **frowns**. She didn't see Max in assembly. It *is* strange. But still – the way Cassandra jumped in, how fast she was to point fingers . . .

'I think it's a bit of a leap to start accusing someone when we don't even know if the trophy is missing,' Ava says, more carefully now.

There's a moment of pause. Cassandra lingers for just a second longer, then turns sharply and walks off, her long ponytail swinging in time with her steps. Her shoes squeak faintly on the polished tiles.

'Let's go and ask Mrs Bell who's got the trophy,' says Jo. 'That will put an end to the mystery right now.'

'Good idea,' says Ava just as the second bell **shrieks** overhead, its high-pitched warning scattering the remaining students.

Jo and Ava are about to head for the admin building when Mrs Campbell, a Year Three teacher, hurries past, a stack of papers tucked under one arm. 'Off to roll call please, kids.'

'But –' Jo objects.

'Now,' Mrs Campbell replies firmly.

Jo and Ava turn back in the direction of their classroom.

Jo chews the inside of her cheek. 'What was all *that* about?' she murmurs.

'Cassandra was acting ***super weird***,' Ava says, glancing behind them. 'She's really got it in for Max.'

Jo nods. 'It makes no sense,' she mutters, biting her lip. 'I hope the trophy turns up soon with a really simple explanation.'

They slide into their seats just as the teacher calls for quiet. Pencil cases zip open, chairs scrape, the school day resumes around them like nothing's wrong.

But Jo has already gone straight back to worrying about the trophy. She knows she won't be able to settle until she has ***solved the mystery*** and the trophy is found.

CHAPTER FIVE

'I get that it just looks like a hunk of metal, but it's more than a trophy,' says Jo as she and Ava head to their trays and swap out their English books for Maths workbooks.

The tray unit creaks as they slide the books in. Around them, the class hums with quiet chatter and chair legs screech into place.

Ava nods, already flipping through her workbook.

'You see, up until last year, Talma Valley had never, ever, won a netball final in the entire history of the school. The basketball team wins every year. They're the reigning champions, but for us, this seemed so far out of our reach. And then somehow, we did it. And it's a big deal.'

Jo pauses to underline something on the top line of her worksheet, but she's not ready to move on yet.

'We'll go ask at recess,' says Ava, eyes still on her book.

'I can't wait in ***suspense*** any longer,' Jo mutters through gritted teeth, gripping her pencil case like it might burst open with answers. 'There's been no announcement. How can the staff leave us hanging like this?'

'I don't think a netball trophy is too high up on the leadership team's agenda,' says Ava. 'Although it *would* be nice to be kept updated.'

Before Jo can reply, their teacher looks up from her laptop.

'Jo, would you like to sit down now?'

Jo slumps into her seat, the legs of her chair scraping **loudly** on the lino floor. She watches the clock tick painfully slowly, willing the bell to ring faster.

The second the recess bell sounds, Jo is up and ***impatiently*** making her way towards the office, motioning for Ava to follow.

The girls slip through the crowd, weaving between groups of kids heading for the playground or the canteen.

The school office is tucked in at the end of the hallway lined with lockers and the trophy cabinet.

There's already a small line of students behind the counter. Jo fidgets behind Sammy holding a note for his teacher and Ivy clutching an ice pack to her elbow. Mrs Bell, behind the desk, takes her time speaking with each one. Jo has always appreciated the time and care Mrs Bell takes with every single student but today . . . today she wishes Mrs Bell wasn't quite so nice!

Jo waits, foot tapping. Ava's arms are folded. The ***hum*** of the photocopier clicks in the corner. Alannah, the work-experience student, is photocopying class sets for Mrs Bell.

‘What would you like me to do with these, Mrs Bell?’ Alannah asks.

‘Alannah, you’ve a wiz,’ beams Mrs Bell. ‘Run those to Mr Campbell in 4C for me, please.’

Alannah gives Jo and Ava a smile before heading off.

Finally, Mrs Bell turns her attention to the girls.

‘Jo? Ava? What can I do for you?’

‘Hi, Mrs Bell,’ Jo says, trying to keep her voice casual. ‘We were just wondering . . . you know the netball championship trophy that Mr Redfern was looking for this morning?’

Mrs Bell’s expression ***flickers***, just for a second.

'Yes, I know the one.'

'Do you know where it is?'

'Mr Redfern said it was maybe being cleaned?' adds Ava.

Mrs Bell pauses, then reaches for a large A3 diary, heavy with pen ink.

'I know, I know, I'm old school,' she says as she spreads open the pages. Mrs Bell flicks through a few pages and runs a finger down a column of dates.

'We do clean the trophies once a year, as silver tends to tarnish,' she says, flipping the page again. 'But that wasn't due to be done until . . .' She squints. 'September.'

Jo steps a little closer. 'So, you don't know where it is?' she presses.

'It's just . . . nobody's saying anything and we have a ***huge game*** this Friday. It'd be good to know what's going on.'

Before Mrs Bell can answer, a noisy group of Year Two kids thunder down the corridor outside. She straightens in her chair, gives them a sharp look through the window, and instantly the volume drops. The footsteps fade.

She glances sideways, checking if anyone else is within earshot, and then leans forward over the desk, lowering her voice.

'I probably shouldn't say this,' she says, 'but . . . it hasn't been found. And from what I've heard, nobody knows where it's gone. Mr Redfern is very unhappy.'

Jo's stomach drops. She turns to Ava, whose mouth tightens into a thin line.

'It really *is* missing,' Ava says quietly.

Mrs Bell nods once. 'Let's hope it turns up soon.'

'But we have to find it . . .' Jo's voice cracks slightly. She's ***shocked*** to realise she might actually cry. Over a trophy. But it's not just a trophy. The trophy really means something.

Mrs Bell softens. 'I can see you're upset, Jo. Look – leave it with me. I'll ask around. Perhaps the cleaner did take it to polish. You never know.'

She offers Jo a ***kind smile***, the kind that grown-ups save for kids when things feel a bit too big.

'Thanks,' Jo says, and she means it.

CHAPTER SIX

For a moment, neither Ava nor Jo says a word. Their footsteps fall in sync.

Then Ava speaks. 'I've got a ***funny feeling***.'

'Same,' Jo replies. Her arms are folded tightly across her chest. 'Something's not adding up.'

'We have ourselves a new mystery.'

Both girls stop walking and look at each other.

'We can solve this, right?' Ava asks.

Jo nods. 'One hundred percent.'

'I mean, we've found missing things before – like ***escaped*** cows and errant mountain-bike riders!'

'And lost suitcases!' Jo adds.

They reach their lockers and grab their recess out of their bags.

'No pressure,' says Jo, 'but we need to wrap this up before the game on Friday. You can't have a district championship without a trophy to present to the winning team – which, by the way, will be us.'

'All we really know is that the trophy is ***officially missing***,' Ava replies. 'It hasn't been sent away to be engraved or polished. It's gone. Mrs Bell was just telling me what I wanted to hear. I don't think the school cleaner has taken it to be cleaned.'

'I can't believe anyone at this school would take the trophy,' says Jo.

'What about the basketball guys?' asks Ava. 'Didn't you say the ***rivalry*** was ***fierce***?'

Jo gives Ava a doubtful glance.

'Okay, maybe not *steal-a-trophy* low,' Ava continues. 'But remember you told me about the time they replaced all of the netballs with basketballs before training?'

Jo snorts. 'That was so annoying.'

Ava nods. 'And what about the sticky bib incident? That sounded kind of ***gross***.'

Jo raises an eyebrow. 'Yes, they sprayed adhesive glue on the backs of our bibs. We were peeling them off our shirts for a week.' She bites into her apple. 'We netball girls aren't completely without blame, though.'

Ava shrugs, grinning. 'What about the great hoop swap everyone talks about?'

Jo laughs. 'We raised the basketball hoops by ten centimetres!'

Ava giggles. 'I'll bet they spent half the session wondering what the heck had happened to their aim. 'And from what I heard, you also may or may not have glitter-bombed their team meeting.'

Jo doubles over now, she's ***laughing*** so hard. 'That was *Tamsin*. But yes. They did have to play with glitter in their hair and it was the best!'

Their giggling is cut short when Max's voice slices through the air, 'I told you, it wasn't me!'

'Looks like Max found Cassandra,' says Jo. 'Or maybe Cassandra found Max.'

Jo instinctively grabs Ava's sleeve and nods towards the back of the building.

'Let's go see what's going on,' Jo whispers.

Ava nods as the two friends follow what sounds like Cassandra and Max locked in a ***heated*** argument.

CHAPTER SEVEN

Tucked in the shade behind a demountable, Cassandra is standing toe-to-toe with Max. Neither of them seems to notice Jo and Ava hovering nearby.

'You were there,' Max hisses at Cassandra, ***frustration*** etched on his face. 'You're the one who keeps bringing me up!'

'You were lurking near the cabinet!' Cassandra snaps. 'It's not my fault if people noticed. And you still haven't said why you weren't in assembly and why you were hanging around *right next to* the trophy cabinet.'

Jo and Ava duck behind a row of lockers. From here, they can't hear every word, but the tone is unmistakable: ***sharp***, ***defensive***, ***accusatory***. A storm building between two stubborn forces.

'Cassandra's really pushing this,' Ava whispers.

'Too hard,' Jo mutters.

'And why weren't *you* in assembly, then?' Max demands.

Cassandra goes bright red and her bottom lip ***trembles***. 'That's personal.'

Then Max's voice rings out again – more tired than angry now. 'So, *you* can have secrets but *I'm* a thief?'

His expression is somewhere between disbelief and disappointment. He turns and stalks off, head low, shoes crunching the loose gravel underfoot.

Cassandra watches him go, arms crossed so tightly she could be holding herself together. Her ponytail swings like a pendulum as she spins around and walks off in the opposite direction, heading straight for the netball courts.

Jo and Ava wait a beat, then step out from behind the building.

'I wondered why neither of them were at assembly,' Jo says.

'Do you really think Max would take our trophy?' asks Ava, brow furrowed. 'I mean, I know there's the netball/basketball rivalry, but that . . .' Her voice trails off as if it's too awful to say out loud.

'Only one way to find out,' says Jo, a new ***determination*** in her face. 'Let's make a plan of attack for solving the case.'

'Good idea!' Ava agrees.

'Remember when we were trying to figure out who sabotaged Dad's hulling machine?'

'Oh yes,' says Ava with a cheeky grin on her face, 'that was a ***tough nut*** to crack.'

Jo rolls her eyes.

'Sorry, go on,' says Ava.

'Well, we put together a list of suspects and interviewed them. And with the missing mountain biker, we followed the clue of the farm gate being left open.'

Ava nods. 'So, in *this* case we need to look carefully at any clues and question people who might have seen something.'

Jo nods. 'Where do we begin?'

Ava pauses, then they both say at once: 'Cassandra?'

'So weird,' Jo says. 'The way she jumped in to accuse Max?

She basically appeared out of nowhere after the bell.'

'And she wasn't at assembly. Did you notice?' Ava warms up to the subject.

'First thing I noticed.'

'But then neither was Max. Perhaps this is all a ***prank*** gone wrong?'

'Let's start with Max,' says Jo. 'Let's go after him before he gets away!'

CHAPTER EIGHT

'Max!' Jo's voice rings out across the courtyard as she breaks into a jog.

She's moving fast, Ava only a few steps behind her. Both girls have to run to catch up to Max. His long strides mean he's already halfway down the side path that leads to the bike racks.

'Wait up!' calls Ava.

Max hears them. Stops. Turns. His face is already set in a ***scowl***.

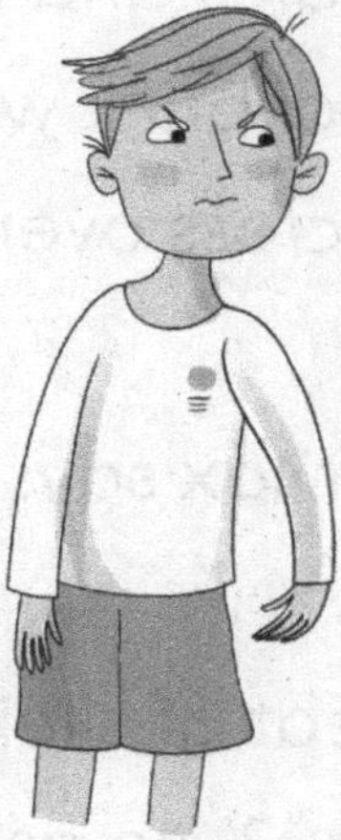

'What?' He's not exactly welcoming, but he doesn't walk away.

'We just want to ask you . . .' Jo struggles to find the right words.

'Can we talk to you for a second?' Ava asks, softer, more cautious.

Max eyes them both for a moment, clearly weighing whether

this is going to be an interrogation or something else. After a long pause, he exhales and leans back against the red-brick wall behind him. His arms cross over his chest like a barrier.

'Fire away,' Max says. 'Cassandra already has.'

There's a beat of silence.

'Are you okay?' Jo asks, her voice gentler now. 'Things between you and Cassandra looked . . . pretty heated.'

Max doesn't answer right away. At first, it looks like he's going to brush it off with ***sarcasm*** or ***frustration*** – his jaw tightens. But then his whole body seems to sag, as though the energy to be annoyed just slips away.

'Oh . . . you heard that?'

Ava nods. Her expression is open, not accusing – just curious, maybe even a little concerned.

'Is there anything you want to tell us?' Jo asks. Her tone is measured. She's trying not to sound like she's ***accusing*** him of anything, but also not letting him off the hook.

Max lets out another sigh – his third in less than a minute.

'*Yes*, I was near the cabinet this morning,' he admits, the words coming slowly. 'But I wasn't doing anything shifty.'

'Okay,' Jo says, and waits. 'We're not accusing you of anything. We just want to rule you out. I mean, you *are* on the basketball team.'

Max shoots her a look.

'Hey – I hate the whole rivalry thing. It started as a ***joke*** but then got totally out of hand. Although, a few of the pranks have been pretty funny . . .'

Jo tilts her head. 'Taking the trophy might've seemed like a fun prank to some people. We get that. But if that's what happened, it's time to come clean.'

Max hesitates. He's clearly reluctant, but something in the way Jo and Ava are standing – waiting, quiet, serious – tells him he might as well just say it.

Then, finally, he speaks.

'Like I said, I was there,' Max murmurs, his voice nearly a whisper now. 'But not for the trophy.' He shifts his weight from one foot to the other. 'Cassandra's locker is along that wall. I was going to leave something for her.'

Jo ***frowns***, completely thrown. 'Wait. What?'

Max doesn't meet their eyes.

'Were you going to prank her?' asks Jo. 'This whole netball/basketball thing . . .'

'I was going to leave her a note.' Max looks down at his feet.

'I was going to tell her I like her, okay?'

The words hang in the air. Jo blinks. This is not what she was expecting to hear.

'You like Cassandra?' Ava blurts, stunned.

Max shrugs one shoulder but still won't look at them.

'She's ***fierce***,' he says quietly. 'I know she acts like I'm the enemy, and yeah, maybe we argue a bit, but I thought maybe . . . I don't know. It was dumb.'

Jo opens her mouth, then closes it again, then finally says, 'Wow.'

Max laughs, but there's no joy in it.

'So, why weren't you in assembly?' asks Jo.

'Oh . . .' Max blushes. 'I was hanging around her locker to put the note inside when nobody was around and she saw me and I kind of ***freaked out*** and went and hid in the boys' toilets.'

'O-kay . . .' says Jo.

'And now everyone thinks I'm a thief.'

'Well . . .' Ava isn't sure what else to say. He's kind of right.

'Here.' Max holds a crumpled note out to the girls.

Jo and Ava lean in to read the scrawled handwriting. Max is telling the truth. He really did write

Cassandra a letter telling her his real feelings for her. Jo feels so bad for him!

'We get the message,' Jo says, handing the letter back. 'We don't need to read it.'

Ava nods beside her. 'We believe you.'

Max finally looks up. There's something raw in his expression – surprise. He studies their faces like he's checking for sarcasm or judgement. But there's none.

'We know you're no trophy thief,' Jo says, meeting his eyes. 'But we'll need your help to prove it.'

CHAPTER NINE

'Weird,' says Jo, frowning. 'She's *always* here at lunch.'

Jo and Ava scan the netball courts. They're full to ***bursting*** with Rose, Kiki, Tamsin and other Wildcats, but Cassandra is not among the players.

Ava squints towards the sports shed. 'There she is!'

Cassandra strides out of the equipment shed with purpose – ponytail swinging, hands shoved in her jacket pockets.

'Come on!' Jo says.

They jog to catch her, but Cassandra ***disappears*** into the main building before they can call out.

The girls enter the building, but there's no sign of Cassandra.

'This way,' says Jo, heading left. They ***furtively*** make their way down the hallway, their backs pressed against the wall. The school is still buzzing, but not crowded – perfect for not being noticed.

'There she is,' Jo whispers. They spot Cassandra again just outside the staffroom. She's talking to Mrs Bell, her expression tense. Then she leaves, heading in the opposite direction.

Jo and Ava edge closer.

'Hi, Mrs Bell,' says Jo.

Mrs Bell smiles. 'Hello, girls. All good?'

'We were just looking for Cassandra,' Ava says quickly.

'Oh! She was here a second ago!' trills Mrs Bell. 'I'm sure you can still catch her.'

'Was she not feeling well?' asks Ava.

'She's fine. No, she was doing exactly what you're doing – trying to figure out where that trophy went,' Mrs Bell says with a ***chuckle***. 'We were just going over what's been checked. Actually, here's Alannah now. I sent her to look through all our trophy supplies. Maybe she can help you.'

'I'm sorry, Jo, I haven't found your trophy,' Alannah says. 'Just lots

of dusty old trophies that need a polish.'

'Thanks anyway,' says Jo.

'I think it's cuppa time, Alannah,' says Mrs Bell. 'See you girls, enjoy your lunch.'

'Thanks, Mrs Bell,' the girls say in unison.

The friends head outside and Ava immediately spots Cassandra.

'That way,' Ava says, pointing.

They follow Cassandra through the library, then out near the art wing. Her head ***swivels***, scanning. She picks up her pace.

'She's doubling back,' Jo mutters.

They trail her from a safe distance. Cassandra ducks behind the kiln room, then ***disappears*** again. Jo and Ava rush to the corner, but she's already crossing the quad, moving fast.

Ava grabs Jo's sleeve. 'Wait.'

Jo stops. 'What?'

'Look at her,' Ava murmurs. 'That's not casually searching. She looks . . .

desperate. She's on some kind of mission.'

Jo and Ava stand back and watch as Cassandra tries the handle of a storeroom.

Locked.

She glances over her shoulder – not at Jo and Ava, but as if she *feels* followed – then hurries into the tech corridor. She peers into a classroom, slips in, then back out like she's checking something ***precise***.

Then she vanishes behind the music block.

'She's looking *everywhere*,' Jo whispers.

They circle the music wing just in time to see Cassandra exit the side door and cross into the sick bay.

She opens a tall cupboard near the door. She leans in, checks quickly, then shuts it again with a frown.

She pauses. Listens. Then ***darts*** back into the hallway.

Before Jo or Ava can get any closer, the bell rings – loud and final.

Students start flooding back indoors and Cassandra melts into the crowd.

Jo and Ava stand frozen in the breezeway.

'We've got to talk to her,' Jo says.

But they have run out of time.

CHAPTER TEN

At the end of the school day, Jo, Ava and the rest of the team head straight to the netball court behind the school. Normally, Jo would be ***buzzing*** to hit the court, already running drills in her head, but today she feels distracted. Her thoughts rotate around one thing: *If Max didn't take the trophy, then who* *did? And why? And* what *is up with Cassandra?*

As they drop their bags beside the court, Jo spots Cassandra tightening her shoelaces. She exchanges a glance with Ava and makes her way over.

'Hey, Cass. Can we talk for a sec? Before we start?'

Cassandra doesn't look up. 'About what?'

'Just . . . the trophy,' Ava says quietly.

Cassandra stands, brushing off her shorts. 'Not now. Training's about to start.'

Jo hesitates. 'After training, then?'

But Cassandra is already jogging towards the centre circle. 'I've got to go straight after,' she calls over her shoulder.

Ava mutters, 'Well, that's not ***suspicious*** at all.'

Jo doesn't answer. She's already watching Cassandra's back, frowning.

The girls chat lightly as they dig out water bottles. Coach Miriam – also Kiki's mum – jogs over from the staff room, clipboard in hand and whistle tucked into her hoodie pocket. Her face lights up as she sees the group forming. They're lucky to have their Wildcats coach also volunteer to train the school team.

She puts down the clipboard and calls the team in. 'Good to see everyone. I know it's been a ***weird*** day,' she says. 'You've all heard the talk about the trophy being misplaced.'

A few girls nod. Cassandra stands slightly apart, jaw tight, eyes flicking towards the school building behind them.

'Do you know something, Coach?' Jo asks.

Coach pauses for a beat, then shakes her head. 'I don't. I've left it with the higher-ups. Our focus needs to be one hundred percent on the game we have this Friday. Trophy or no trophy, we have a final to win. East Ridge are in fighting form this season, so it's going to take everything we've got – which is a **strong defence**, **excellent communication** and **sharp shooting**. Am I right?'

Coach is met with a chorus of:

'Yes, Coach!'

'We've got this!'

'Take that, East Ridge!'

Jo lets out a slow breath. Coach is right. Whatever's going on with the trophy, it's not going to help them win on Friday.

'All right,' Coach continues. 'Warm-up laps – two around the court. Then we'll stretch and run through quick rotations. Let's go.'

The team takes off. Kiki leads, Ava beside her. There's a little chatter, but not the usual jokes or bursts of laughter. Jo settles into a steady rhythm, scanning the group. Everyone's putting in effort – no one's slacking – but it still feels . . . ***strained***.

Pull yourself together, Jo, she tells herself. Every training session before a final is tense. She's reading too much into it.

But there's no escaping that something is definitely wrong with Cassandra. She fumbles a stretch, stares into space, reties her shoelace twice.

Jo leans into a side stretch and **sneaks** a glance at Ava. Ava meets her eye and gives the tiniest shake of her head. She's seen it too.

Drills begin. Chest passes. Shoulder passes. In groups of three, Jo, Ava and Rose work smoothly.

On the other side of the court, Cassandra and Amaya are out of sync. Cassandra overthrows a pass. Then underthrows the next. She mutters an apology under her breath. Amaya keeps glancing at her like she's trying to figure out what's going on but she's afraid to ask.

Coach walks through the groups, giving feedback. Jo notes she doesn't say anything to Cassandra but gives her space.

The team breaks into half-court plays. Jo slips into Goal Defence. Tamsin takes Centre. Things move well enough, but Cassandra's still not herself. She calls for the ball, then ***freezes*** mid-step and ***fumbles*** the catch. She throws a hasty pass to Kiki that sails wide.

'Reset,' Coach says. Her tone's calm, steady.

They run the play again. And again. Each time, a little better. But it's not flowing like it should.

After twenty minutes, Coach brings them in.

'Okay, team, that's enough for today. You've got the skills. We're all a little hyped and that's just nerves. We need to channel those nerves and use them to our **advantage**. Lots of early nights, good food and plenty of fluids over the next few days.'

As bags are picked up and water bottles repacked, Jo and Ava fall into step towards the school gate.

They wait until they're clear of the court before Jo murmurs, 'Did you see her?'

Ava nods. 'Something's off.'

Jo bites her lip. 'She's trying, but it's like she's somewhere else. If we're going to ***fix*** the team before Friday, we've got to figure out what's going on with her.'

CHAPTER ELEVEN

Jo lies on her bed. Billie is curled up at her feet like a furry hot water bottle.

Jo plays the morning's events over and over in her mind but she still can't make sense of who took the trophy. And, *why*?

Ava's name lights up on Jo's phone screen.

Ava: *Can't stop thinking about the trophy.*

Jo: *Me neither. Want to call?*

Ava: *Yep.*

Jo answers before the second ring.

'Hi,' Ava says. Her voice is quiet. 'So . . . Cassandra.'

'I know!' Jo sits up. 'I was thinking about her too.'

They both fall silent for a beat.

'Do you think she took it?' Ava asks.

Jo hesitates. 'I don't know. I just don't see why. She ***loves netball*** and she loves the team.'

'She doesn't like Max!'

'She *really* doesn't like him,' Jo agrees. 'Which is pretty sad given that we now know he likes her.'

Jo sits up, Billie shifting slightly across the bed covers. 'But what if she likes him too? Or she thinks he doesn't take her seriously? Like, she wants to impress him but she's going about it in the wrong way.'

Ava snorts. 'You think Cassandra likes *Max*?'

'I don't know,' Jo admits. 'I mean, anything's possible.'

Ava goes quiet for a second. 'I wonder . . . It would explain her OTT behaviour.'

Jo nods, though Ava can't see it.

'So, what do we do?' Ava asks.

'We follow the clues,' says Jo. 'We keep asking questions until we figure out ***the truth***.'

'You sound just like a real detective!' laughs Ava.

Jo puts Ava on speaker, then opens their group chat and starts typing a message to Cassandra. She reads it aloud to Ava before she posts: *Hey Cass. Can we meet before school tomorrow? Just us. Netball stuff. 8am outside the court?*

A pause. Then both girls see the reply **flash** back.

Sure.

Ava lets out a slow breath. 'Okay. Let's see what she says.'

'Night.'

'Night.'

Jo strokes Billie's ears. 'Wish we could bring you, girl. You've cracked bigger mysteries than this.'

Billie snores softly in reply.

CHAPTER TWELVE

'Thanks, Dad!' Ava gives her dad a wave as she steps out of the car.

'Have a great day,' he calls and he toots the car horn as he drives away.

'I might have forgotten to tell Dad we are planning to ***interrogate*** a suspect in a theft!' says Ava.

Jo laughs. 'Need-to-know basis at this stage.'

The school grounds are unusually quiet. It's too early for the usual buzz of students. A faint mist still curls around the edges of the oval, and the air smells like damp bark.

Cassandra is waiting, her school bag at her feet. She stands ***stiffly***, like she's been there a while, shifting her weight from one foot to the other. Her arms are folded tightly across her chest.

'Morning,' she says.

'Hey,' Jo replies. 'Thanks for meeting us.'

'Sure!' she says pertly. Then she continues in a quieter tone, 'Is it about my playing at training last night? Sorry, I was all over the place.'

Jo shakes her head. 'No way! You're an ***amazing player***. We all have off nights.'

Cassandra looks relieved. Her shoulders drop slightly, and she lets out a small breath she must have been holding.

'So, what's up?'

Jo glances at Ava, who nods slightly. Jo steps forward.

'Cassandra . . . we can tell something's up. You're not yourself.'

'And the whole trophy thing . . .' adds Ava.

'What about it?' Cassandra says sharply. Her tone is defensive, too fast, and Jo catches the slight narrowing of her eyes.

Jo jumps in. 'You were very quick to blame Max.'

'Oh, *Max*!' Cassandra rolls her eyes. Her voice sharpens again, but there's a flicker of something else in her expression – maybe embarrassment.

Jo and Ava wait her out. The silence grows, filled only by the occasional call of a crow and the distant **clatter** of bins being wheeled to the kerb near the canteen.

Cassandra hesitates, then sighs and turns away. 'Okay. Fine.'

She kicks at a crack in the asphalt, then finally blurts out – 'I took the trophy.'

'What?!' Jo is ***incredulous***.

'Just hear me out,' says Cassandra. 'Look, Max has been acting all smug, and you know how he teases us about how netball isn't a real sport, and I saw him near my locker and then . . . the cabinet door was open and I thought I'd just take it and then it could be funny if people thought it was him . . .'

'Not really,' says Jo.

'I know, it's not funny at all. I'm *so* embarrassed,' says Cassandra, running a hand down her long ponytail. 'I know I shouldn't have done it!'

'Well, I mean, you can just put it

back and then everything will be fine,' says Ava.

'That's the thing! I already did!' says Cassandra, her gaze intense. Her words come in a ***rush*** now, like she's been holding them in for too long.

'I don't understand,' says Ava.

Cassandra sighs. 'I took the trophy out of the cabinet to set Max up, but then he just appeared. He should have been in assembly and then I worried that he'd seen me take it, so I freaked out and put it straight back.'

'You put the trophy back in the cabinet?' asks Jo. Her brow furrows and she crosses her arms slowly.

'But now the trophy's disappeared?' adds Ava.

'You've got to believe me!' Cassandra looks up at them, panicked. 'I didn't mean for any of this to happen. It's all got out of hand. I know I did the wrong thing trying to set Max up like that, but I am *not* the reason the trophy is missing.'

There's something about her tone of voice and how she seems genuinely ***distressed*** that makes Jo believe Cassandra is telling the truth. She exchanges a look with Ava and can tell she's thinking the same thing.

'We believe you,' Jo says.

'But someone *has* taken it,' says Ava.

'Do you think Max would have?' Cassandra asks in a low voice.

'No,' both girls say firmly. 'We've cleared Max. That's step one.'

'And step two?' Cassandra asks.

Jo's eyes narrow with ***new resolve***. 'We find out who actually took the trophy. Before the final.'

Cassandra nods. 'Whatever you need. I'll help.'

'We hoped you'd say that,' says Jo. 'We've already got one helper, so between the four of us we should get to the bottom of this in no time.'

'Who's the other helper?' asks Cassandra.

Jo and Ava grin. 'You know him.'

At that moment, Max rounds the corner, hands in his pockets, trying to look casual and failing miserably. His backpack bumps against his hip with each step. He spots the group and slows.

Cassandra's smile ***vanishes***. 'You've got to be kidding.'

Max stops a few metres away. 'I didn't know she'd be here,' he mutters to Jo.

Cassandra glances sideways at Max, then back at Jo. 'Oh, come on . . .'

'She better not try to ***blame me*** again,' says Max under his breath.

Jo and Ava exchange a look that says this is going to be . . . interesting. 'Let's continue this at The Milk Bar,' says Jo. 'We've got just enough time before school. Let's go!'

CHAPTER THIRTEEN

'Yuuuum!' Jo says as she steps through the door of The Milk Bar.

It is deliciously warm inside and smells of freshly baked treats.

Jo holds the door open for the others.

Larry, the owner, looks up from behind the counter where he's arranging the day's muffins. 'Usuals?'

‘Thanks, Larry!’ Jo grins. Larry knows everybody. The Junior Wildcats usually come here after a game and Jo is pretty sure that Max’s team, The Falcons, do too.

They head straight to the back booth. The vinyl seats let out a polite squeak as they slide in.

Larry gets to work pouring milk into tall glasses and scooping generous ***blobs*** of ice cream into the blender. He doesn’t need to ask flavours – Jo’s is always chocolate; Ava used to order chocolate until she tasted Larry’s vanilla malt; Max’s is strawberry; and Cassandra gets banana.

When the milkshakes arrive, thick and topped with striped paper straws, Jo pulls a napkin from the holder and flattens it on the table like it's a ***tactical blueprint***.

'Okay,' she says, lowering her voice even though the only other customer is Frank Cooper reading his paper in the corner. 'Recap: The trophy was taken some time before assembly. Cassandra removed it but then put it back – somebody else has taken it.'

Ava sips her shake. 'And we've cleared Max. He was too busy . . . doing other things . . .'

Max stares into his glass. 'And moving the subject on, please . . .'

Jo clears her throat. 'Right. So. Two main problems. One: We don't know who took the trophy. Two: We don't know why.'

Ava leans forward. 'What if it was a teacher? Mrs Bell said it's not normal for something to go missing like this. And Mrs Jensen was the one who went looking for it at assembly and came back empty-handed.'

At the mention of Mrs Jensen, Cassandra ***shudders***.

'She told me once that my hair looked like it had been dragged through a hedge backwards,' says Max, sipping his shake with feeling.

Jo glances at Max's unruly hair and decides not to say anything.

'She called me "alarmingly disorganised",' says Ava.

'She's not wrong,' Jo says **cheerfully**. 'But she's also the most involved with the display case. She's the one who polishes everything

and logs what's in there. If anyone noticed something ***strange***, it'd be her.'

Cassandra frowns. 'You think she took it?'

'Not really,' Jo admits. 'But we need to speak to her if only to clear her name.'

'Jo's right,' says Ava. 'For now, she's our only lead. You both saw the trophy just before she came out alone and announced to the school that it was missing. Either someone else acted very quickly with no witnesses – or it was Mrs Jensen.'

'No way we all go together,' Max says. 'Too suspicious.'

Jo points her straw at them. 'Perfect. Split the team.'

'Agreed,' Cassandra says, twisting her straw in her milkshake. 'Report back to us afterwards.'

'And what will you two be doing while we chat to Mrs Jensen?' Ava asks.

Before Max can answer, Cassandra jumps in – 'I'm going to be doing netball training every spare second I have.'

'I could help you, if you like?' says Max.

'You?' Cassandra looks at him. 'Play netball?'

'I'll have you know I'm a pretty good basketball player,' says Max.

'Yes, but are you any good at netball?'

'Only one way to find out!'

'It's a deal!'

Cassandra looks sideways at Max and smiles.

Momentarily ***emboldened***, Max holds out his milkshake. 'I'd like to say something for the record. I have nothing but the highest respect for netball, the game, the players. I wish half our team were as good as you girls. So, let's drop this whole rivalry thing. To solving the mystery.'

They hold out their milkshakes and clink glasses.

'We just need to bring Jane and Tamsin up to speed,' Jo says, then takes a sip of her milkshake. 'And then ***Operation Trophy Hunt*** is officially on.'

CHAPTER FOURTEEN

Jo and Ava spot Mrs Jensen locking up the PE storeroom just before the morning bell. She's balancing a clipboard in one hand and swinging the padlock shut with the other. As always, she's dressed in tracksuit pants and a sports shirt, her whistle looped around her neck.

'Mrs Jensen?' Jo calls. 'Have you got a minute?'

Mrs Jensen turns, surprised but not bothered. 'Sure, girls. What's going on?'

Jo steps forward. 'It's about the missing netball trophy.'

Mrs Jensen's expression doesn't change as she leans casually against the brick wall. 'Yes?'

'Well, we've been thinking about it and we put together a timeline of events from that morning,' stammers Jo.

'A timeline?'

Jo nods. 'It's standard procedure in a ***detective's playbook***.'

Mrs Jensen suppresses a small smile. 'Go on.'

'We have ***witnesses*** who can place the trophy in the cabinet as late as after assembly had started.'

'This is useful information,' says Mrs Jensen. 'When exactly?'

'Around the time the school anthem played.'

'So, that's a really small window before you came out to grab it,' Ava continues. 'And we wondered if you could talk us through what you saw. Any detail could be helpful for our ***investigation***.'

Mrs Jensen lets out a breath, thinking. 'Not much to tell. Mr Redfern asked me to grab it, so I walked out of the hall to the display cabinet. But it actually took me a moment to realise it was missing. I stood there blinking at the glass, wondering if I'd somehow missed it. All those trophies look the same when you're not paying attention.'

'Did anything else look out of place or unusual?' asks Jo.

'No,' Mrs Jensen says, shaking her head, 'not that I can recall. I poked my head into the office, but it was just Alannah packing boxes and I didn't want to keep the assembly waiting.'

'Anything else at all? No matter how irrelevant it seems?' Jo presses.

Mrs Jensen pauses, glancing upward. 'The floor near the office was a bit slippery, actually. Freshly mopped, I do remember that.'

'Right,' says Jo.

'I figured it'd turn up by recess,' Mrs Jensen adds. 'Didn't expect it to become a ***full-blown mystery***.'

The bell rings.

'Well, thanks,' Ava says.

'We appreciate you speaking to us,' Jo adds.

'Okay, detectives, do I have the all clear?' Mrs Jensen jokes but she doesn't wait around for an answer. She gives them a quick smile and heads off towards the staff building.

Jo exhales. 'Well . . . that didn't really get us anywhere.'

They start walking slowly towards their classroom.

Jo bites her lip. 'You don't think . . . Mrs Jensen would've taken it herself, do you?'

'Why would she?' Ava replies.

'I don't know.' Jo frowns. 'Maybe she's not thrilled about Coach Miriam taking over training the team this year? I mean, as **scary** as Mrs Jensen is, she was the one who got us through to the finals last season. What if she's upset her role has changed?'

Ava raises an eyebrow. 'That's a pretty big leap.'

‘Just a theory,’ Jo replies.

They keep walking. A few younger students race past shouting about handball.

‘I just don’t want to rule anything out yet,’ Jo murmurs. ‘Something still feels off.’

They are almost at their classroom when the second bell rings. Behind them, the corridor returns to silence and suddenly a bright yellow trolley blocks their path. It is stacked with paper towel rolls and a spray bottle that smells strongly of eucalyptus.

‘Oops – sorry!’ Ava says, steadying herself.

‘All good, girls!’ says Mr Lloyd, the school cleaner who has just stepped out of the PE storeroom. He expertly steers the trolley towards the breezeway. He's wearing his usual navy polo shirt and cap, and there's a faint smear of floor polish on his elbow. A small speaker is clipped to the side of his belt, playing old-school jazz at a low, boppy volume.

He hums along, doing a little ***two-step shuffle*** as he moves.

Jo pauses. A thought clicks into place.

'Hey, Mr Lloyd, were you on shift yesterday morning? When the netball trophy went missing?'

He stops, one hand on the trolley handle. 'Yeah, I was. Why?'

'Did you see the trophy in the cabinet?' Jo asks. 'Like, was it still there when you were mopping the floors?'

Mr Lloyd squints upward like he's scrolling back through his memory, still tapping a ***slow rhythm*** against the trolley with one hand. 'Pretty sure it was. I mop that corridor every morning. I remember wiping near the cabinet and noticing the door was a bit ajar – not wide open, just not clicked shut properly.'

Jo and Ava exchange a glance.

'So, the trophy was definitely still in there when you mopped?' Ava asks.

'Yeah,' he says. 'I'm no netball expert, but I remember seeing it – the silver and gold one, right?'

Jo nods quickly. 'That's the one.'

'Well, then, yep. It was there. I'd bet my mop on it.'

'Thanks, Mr Lloyd,' Jo says. 'You've been really helpful.'

'Anytime,' he says, wheeling the trolley forward again. 'Just don't tell anyone I'm the ***new school detective***. I've got too much work as it is.'

As he rolls away, the jazz music fades with him.

Jo turns to Ava, her voice low and urgent. 'That's it. The trophy was still there when he mopped,' she says, trying not to sound too excited. 'But it was gone by the time Mrs Jensen came out. That's only a few minutes, if that.'

Ava's eyes narrow. 'Someone acted really quickly.'

Jo nods slowly. 'Someone's hiding something.'

'Wait up!'

Cassandra's voice cuts in as she jogs towards them, netball under one arm, cheeks flushed. Max trails behind, wiping sweat from his brow and looking ***mildly confused***.

'What's going on?' Cassandra asks. 'We just finished a round of shooting drills. Did you find out anything new?'

'We might have,' Ava says, turning to them.

Jo quickly fills them in – Mr Lloyd, the confirmed sighting of the trophy and the few moments of **opportunity** before Mrs Jensen came out.

Max whistles low. 'So, Mrs Jensen says it was already gone, but Mr Lloyd's saying it wasn't?'

'Exactly,' Jo says. 'It was there when he cleaned. Gone by the time Mrs Jensen came back empty-handed during assembly.'

'Do you think she took it?' Max asks.

'I just don't see why she would,' says Jo. 'But if she's involved, we need to know what she's up to.'

'What do we do now?' Cassandra asks.

Jo looks around at the group. Her eyes sharpen. 'We watch her. Nothing creepy, but after all, what do we really know about her?'

'What do we really know about any teacher?' says Cassandra.

'Information gathering,' says Jo. 'We need to know *everything* about her, what she eats, what she does when she's not at school. In other words – *who is Mrs Jensen?*'

'Do we need ***codenames***?' Max asks, totally serious.

Jo tilts her head. 'That's a great idea!'

'Okay then,' Max says, sitting up straighter. 'I'm ***Falcon***.'

'You don't get to pick your own name,' Jo says.

'Too late,' Max grins. 'I'm already emotionally attached.'

Cassandra rolls her eyes but can't help smiling. 'Fine. I'm ***Cipher***.'

'Love it,' Ava nods. 'Mystery vibes. Suits you.'

'You're ***Echo***,' Jo says to her. 'You pick up everything no one else notices.'

'What about you?' Ava asks.

Jo pauses. ***'Pecan.'***

Max blinks. 'Like . . . the nut?'

'She *is* a little nutty,' deadpans Ava.

'Hard shell. Excellent under pressure. A little weird,' Jo says firmly.

There's a beat of silence, then they all burst out laughing.

The four of them huddle closer. The plan is forming. It's time for some ***proper surveillance***.

CHAPTER FIFTEEN

'Has Max messaged yet?' Ava asks Jo for the fifth time in ten minutes.

The girls are waiting for Max to give them the go-ahead that Mrs Jensen is exiting the school.

Jo checks her phone. '*Action!* Max just saw her leave the staffroom. She's heading for the front gate now.'

Ava's eyes light up. 'Let's go.'

They slip their phones away and weave past the last trickle of students heading to buses. Jo keeps her head low as they cross the basketball courts.

'There,' she mutters.

Mrs Jensen walks ***briskly*** ahead of them, bag slung over one shoulder, clipboard under her arm. She's still in her PE uniform, wearing her usual navy polo and joggers, whistle looped loosely around her neck.

Jo and Ava keep their distance. Just two girls walking home from school. Nothing to see here.

'I feel like we're in a spy movie,' Ava whispers.

'Minus the ***fast cars*** and ***cool gadgets***,' Jo mutters.

'And snacks,' Ava adds. 'Why do spies never eat?'

They follow Mrs Jensen out the back school gate and across the park. She's heading in the opposite direction from town. It's all suburban houses lined with gum trees.

Jo hears the sound of footsteps behind them. Then a giggle and a voice says, 'Shh.'

It's Max and Cassandra. The four friends gather together.

'Anything?' asks Max.

Jo shakes her head. 'No. So, we just keep tailing her, I guess?'

Mrs Jensen turns down a side street, past a row of older houses with wide verandahs and blooming camellias. Jo slows as she spots a white gate swing open.

'Number twenty-two,' Max reads softly from the letterbox.

They duck behind a low hedge across the street, ***crouching*** just enough to keep themselves unseen but still with a view of Mrs Jensen's house. Number 22 is a pretty, whitewashed cottage with a tin roof. The front garden is an explosion of colour. A small statue of a frog wearing sunglasses sits in the middle of a birdbath.

Mrs Jensen disappears up the path and through the screen door. It clatters shut behind her.

The friends wait.

'What now?' asks Cassandra.

'Like proper spies, we wait,' says Jo.

They wait. Then wait some more. Ava starts chewing on a leaf she pulled off the hedge.

'Ava, what are you *doing*?'

'It looked edible.'

'You're going to ***poison*** yourself. Stop being a goat.'

A few minutes later, the front door opens. Mrs Jensen steps out wearing the same navy joggers but a different top, an old camp tee with faded writing across the back. She's holding gardening gloves and a small metal trowel.

Jo stiffens. 'Wait. What's she doing?'

'She's got a trowel,' Max whispers. 'Is she . . . ***digging something up***?'

The friends exchange a glance, eyes wide.

'The trophy?' Jo murmurs. 'She's going to dig it up!'

Jo knows it doesn't make any sense for Mrs Jensen to bury a trophy, but stranger things have happened.

Mrs Jensen bends to inspect a planter box. She slips on the gloves and starts weeding, moving methodically along the row of herbs and flowers. She pulls out a few stragglers, then gently presses the soil back down. No ***suspicious*** hole digging.

'She's . . . gardening,' says Cassandra.

Jo lets out a breath. 'Okay. She's not burying stolen treasure.'

'She's growing snow peas,' Max says, spotting the curling green tendrils along a bamboo frame.

Mrs Jensen moves to another bed, kneeling to thin out a patch of leafy greens.

They stay watching from behind the hedge.

A bee lands on Ava's sleeve. She freezes. 'Jo. Jo. Am I being swarmed?'

Jo doesn't look. 'One bee does not count as a swarm.'

'It's making eye contact.'

Jo finally glances over. 'It's on your *sleeve*. It doesn't have eyes. Just calm down.'

Ava swats it away and immediately regrets it. 'Okay,

maybe we aren't cut out for field work.'

'Speak for yourself,' Jo says, eyes still locked on the garden.

'Not what I expected,' Ava murmurs.

Jo nods. Not what she expected at all.

CHAPTER SIXTEEN

Billie lies stretched out under the gum tree that shades the court. Her eyebrows ***twitch*** back and forth as she watches the group like she's keeping score.

Jo has her work cut out for her. Even though her home court is small, a game of three-on-three means every player is working all the time.

She passes to Ava, who catches the ball cleanly and tries for a shot, but Max's height is in his favour. He easily intercepts and takes a step before making a low pass to Cassandra. Cassandra is ***fast***. She has really got her mojo back since training with Max. She could try for a shot but she's a team player, so she dodges Jane and fires the ball straight into Tamsin's outstretched arms. It's a clean shot for Tamsin.

Jo groans. 'Whose idea was it to have the three tallest players on the same team?'

'Not my fault if Billie chose the teams,' shrugs Tamsin.

'Hey Billie, your sniff test is a little glitchy!' Jo calls to Billie. Billie responds with a tail thump in the dust.

'That was actually a ***solid pivot***, before,' Tamsin says to Max. 'You're getting the hang of it.'

'Thanks,' says Max, puffing slightly. 'Best home set-up ever, Jo. Wish I had room for one of these.'

'Dad and my brothers made it after I nearly wrecked the shed wall practising one summer,' says Jo.

'We've got Billie as a great supporter,' says Cassandra.

'And walnut harvesters for background noise,' Ava adds.

Jo laughs. 'You haven't lived until you've written a science report during a nut sort.'

They keep the ball moving – pass, pivot, shoot. Max fumbles a catch, then recovers and tries a ***spin move*** that looks impressive . . . until he instinctively bounces the ball.

Everyone freezes.

Max winces. 'Still not allowed to bounce it, huh?'

'Still netball,' Jo says, scooping it up. 'Nice footwork, though.'

'Feels unnatural,' Max mutters. He shoots but the ball sails way overhead and lands down among a row of walnut trees. Billie trots over to sniff the ball.

'What was that?' asks Cassandra.

'I can't get my head around not having a backboard. I mean, there's nothing to bounce the ball off when you shoot!' says Max.

'Duh!' says Jane. 'You actually have to have skill.'

Max pulls a face. 'Ouch.'

Jane laughs. 'I'm only ***teasing***. I love basketball.'

Jo retrieves the ball and they take the opportunity to have a break. The sun slips low behind the trees, turning everything amber. Billie checks to see if any food will be available and sinks back down in her spot when it's clear it's just a water break.

'So, our trophy hunt has come to a bit of a ***dead end***. What have we found out about Mrs Jensen?' Jo asks.

'Her desk has a rotating collection of laminated motivational quotes,' Ava says. 'Today's was: *Champions don't complain, they adjust.*'

Max whistles. 'That's intense.'

'I think it's kind of cool,' Jane says. 'Like she's coaching herself all day.'

'Mr Harding says she used to coach all the regional squads,' Tamsin adds. 'She only stepped back when Mr Redfern restructured the PE department.'

'So, she was . . . demoted?' Cassandra asks.

'Sort of. She used to run everything. Now she runs sport classes across K to 6 but no outside coaching.'

'That's got to sting,' Max says. 'Imagine being benched after running the whole show.'

'She also drinks three peppermint teas before lunch,' Jane says. 'The teabags were lined up in a ceramic tray.'

Ava opens her notebook. 'Tamsin and I emptied her bin –'

'It wasn't as ***gross*** as it sounds,' Tamsin adds.

'– and found a receipt from Saturday morning. She went to that garden centre on the highway.

Bought fertiliser, a punnet of petunias – and a sausage roll.'

Max grins. 'So, she's hardcore and has a green thumb. Respect.'

'She's married but has no kids,' Jo says. 'And Cassandra found out she's in the choir at the community hall.'

'They're doing *Les Mis* this year,' Cassandra nods. 'She sings alto.'

Jo raises an eyebrow. 'That . . . actually explains a lot.'

'So, we know her tea preference, her musical history and that she gardens on weekends,' Max says. 'But none of it screams ***trophy thief***.'

'True,' Ava says. 'But it builds a picture. She's disciplined, proud and definitely the kind of person who notices when something's out of place.'

'And maybe the kind of person who doesn't like being sidelined,' Jo says quietly.

'I used to be so scared of her, but she grows her own snow peas,' says Ava with wonder.

'And drinks herbal tea, not coffee,' adds Jane.

'She mulches and her recycling is on point,' adds Tamsin.

'She's a good person,' says Max, nodding.

They sit quietly for a moment. The only sound is Billie's tail brushing against the dirt behind them until a car coming up the long driveway causes her to jump up and bark.

'That'll be my mum,' Cassandra says and stands up. 'Ready to go?'

'Yeah. Thanks again for the lift,' says Max.

'It's the least I could do after all the things I said about you,' Cassandra replies quietly. She holds out a hand to help Max stand. 'I'm sorry.'

Max accepts her hand and she pulls him up. They shake hands.

'Friends?' asks Cassandra.

'Friends,' agrees Max.

Jo and the others exchange a glance.

Cassandra looks at the others and blushes. She changes the subject.

'The final's tomorrow and we have no ***championship trophy*** to present, but somehow it doesn't seem as important as it did.'

'So, what do we do?' asks Jane.

Jo stands too, brushing gravel from her hands.

'I think we get an early night,' says Jo. 'Trophy or no trophy, we've got a ***grand final*** to win!'

CHAPTER SEVENTEEN

Dinner's on the table when Jo comes in from the backyard, cheeks flushed, hair stuck to the back of her neck. Billie trails in behind her, tail swishing, and ***collapses*** under the table like she's played a quarter herself.

'Good training session?' her dad asks, passing her a glass of water.

'Billie thinks so,' Jo says, flopping into her chair. 'We're as ready as we'll ever be.'

Her mum brings over a tray of roasted veggies while her brother Robert, sleeves rolled up, carves the garlic bread with **enthusiasm**. Jo's other brother James has already demolished half his plate.

'Big game tomorrow, little sis,' Robert says, grinning. 'What's the plan?'

'Play hard. Stick together. Ignore the fact that we have no trophy,' Jo says, helping herself to a ladle full of steaming veggies.

'It's still missing?' her mum says, surprised.

Jo nods. 'It's just . . . gone. No leads. No answers.'

There's a pause as forks clink against plates.

'But aren't you and Ava ***seasoned detectives***?' James asks with a mouth full of garlic bread.

'Gross, James!' Jo pulls a face. What was it with older brothers? Both James and Robert could turn any situation into a gross fest.

James just shrugs.

'We've been through everything,' Jo tells her family. 'We interviewed the cleaner and Mrs Bell, we trawled through bins, and we now know that Mrs Jensen weeds her snow peas.'

'I remember Mrs Jensen,' Robert laughs. 'I didn't know she was into snow peas!'

'She gardens. And sings in a choir. And drinks peppermint tea. And keeps every laminated motivational quote ever printed.'

'She sounds like a legend,' says her dad.

'She kind of is. We thought she was ***crabby*** and ***strict***, but really . . . she's just someone who quietly gets on with things. Even after being pushed aside.'

Her mum nods. 'She sounds like someone worth having on your side.'

Billie lets out a quiet snuffle from under the table.

'We've been so caught up in solving the ***mystery***,' Jo continues, 'but maybe the mystery doesn't matter as much as we thought. Maybe it's not about proving something. Maybe it's just about showing up and playing our hearts out.'

James throws a bread crust across the table. 'You're getting deep, Jo.'

She grins. 'Well, it *is* the night before the grand final.'

'You're right, though,' her dad says. 'Sometimes the win isn't about what's on the scoreboard.'

'Now *you're* getting deep!' Jo laughs.

Jo leans back in her chair. Tomorrow is game day. And for the first time all week, the trophy isn't the thing taking up space in her head. It's the team. The game.

Jo raises her glass. 'To whatever happens tomorrow.'

Everyone clinks water and juice.

Billie sighs under the table, like she knows the speech is over.

And just like that, Jo feels ***ready***.

CHAPTER EIGHTEEN

East Ridge Public's team is already warming up, jogging steady laps around the oval in ***tight formation*** – focused, fit and strong. They look like a team fiercely determined to take back the championship.

The Year Six classes are filing in with their teachers, buzzing with excitement. Some are waving paper flags hastily painted in school colours.

On the other side of the court, folding chairs have been set up in neat rows for parents. Jo spots her dad and mum. Billie lies between them, her head between her paws and her lead tied loosely to the leg of a chair.

Jo catches sight of Ava's parents a few rows behind, sitting close together, thermoses in hand. Ava gives them a wave and they beam back ***proudly***.

The basketball boys have gone all out. Max holds up a sign that reads 'GO TALMA' in giant block letters. The L is slightly crooked, but it's the thought that counts. Jo waves to them, ***impressed*** and ***grateful*** for their support.

Tamsin and Cassandra are bouncing on their toes. Jane finishes her stretches and gives Jo a quick thumbs-up.

Coach Miriam's voice cuts through the chatter. 'All right, girls – let's huddle!'

They form a circle.

'We've trained. We've worked. We've got the talent and the ***teamwork***,' Coach says, eyes scanning each of them. 'So, go out there, back yourselves and stick to your opponent like glue.'

'We don't need a trophy to be a team,' says Jo firmly. 'We just need each other.'

She's about to walk into position when Mr Redfern strides onto the court. He's sporting a new pair of black skinny jeans and black street shoes, but he's paired the look with a shirt and tie. He is moving fast with a serious expression and something tucked under his arm.

Coach Miriam looks up, puzzled.

Mr Redfern lifts the object high above his head and it catches the light in the early morning sun.

It's the **championship trophy**.

Cheers erupt from the crowd.

'Before we begin,' he says, loud enough for everyone to hear, 'I'm pleased to announce that the missing netball trophy has been found.'

He places it on the presentation table beside the scorer's bench. It gleams.

Even from where she's standing, Jo can tell that's not the real trophy.

It's close, but Jo knows the small scratch in the handle and the dent at the base from when Jane dropped it. This one's brand new.

Behind the scorer's table, Mrs Jensen stands with her arms folded and a perfectly unreadable expression. She catches Jo's eye and gives the smallest nod.

And then Jo gets it. 'Mrs Jensen had a replica made so we'd still have a trophy,' she whispers to Ava.

'It's actually kind of ***genius***,' Ava whispers back. 'Respect.'

'We playing, or what?' Tamsin grins.

Jo nods to Ava, then turns back to the others.

'Let's go win this thing,' she says.

Coach Miriam claps. 'Positions!'

Jo jogs to her place at Goal Defence. Ava lines up at Wing Attack. The whistle blows.

The ***grand final*** begins.

CHAPTER NINETEEN

Jo snaps to attention. East Ridge's Goal Attack is fast. She's already moving back and forth and looking sharp. Jo remembers her from the semi-final. She rarely misses.

But Talma Valley holds their own.

Ava drives the ball forward like it's stitched to her hands. She ***zips*** past defenders, finds Jane at Centre, and then suddenly – Cassandra is open.

'Now!' Jo yells.

The pass flies. Cassandra ***snatches*** it mid-air, lands solidly and shoots.

The ball arcs, spins, drops.

1–0 to Talma Valley.

The cheer from the sideline erupts. Max is practically levitating. Billie barks, getting caught up in the energy from the crowd.

East Ridge reset with frightening speed. Their passes don't fumble. Their shooters don't hesitate.

Soon, it's 2–1 to East Ridge and then 3–1.

The Talma Valley team comes in hot and slightly deflated at quarter-time.

'How many extra practices do you think they have a week?' Ava ***grumbles***. 'Five? Ten?'

'Their GD's like a wall,' Cassandra says, shaking her arms out. 'I can't get past her.'

Coach Miriam calls for calm. 'You've got this. Talk to each other.'

And soon they're back in the game. Jo breathes deeply. Every part of her is tingling, focused on her form. The East Ridge shooter tries to sneak around, but Jo holds her space, arms held high.

Intercept.

She bats the ball clean and it lands in Tamsin's hands.

From here they find a ***rhythm*** and things begin to move in their favour.

Ava to Jane. Jane to Cassandra. Cassandra back to Ava.

Goal.

3–2.

It's a battle but they're calling well and finding the openings for passes.

Cassandra, who's been jittery all week, plays like she has channelled every ounce of stress into pure focus. Her footwork is fast and she seems to be everywhere, all at once.

By half-time, the score is 4–3 with Talma Valley in the lead.

They regroup on the bench, gulping water, red-faced and determined. Jo glances over at her parents and Billie. Her dad gives her a thumbs-up and she is sure Billie offers a grin.

'You're doing it,' Coach Miriam says. 'Just keep your heads. Stay tight on defence. Trust each other.'

Second half.

East Ridge are throwing everything they've got at this.

But Talma Valley are ***faster*** now. Working smarter, not harder.

Jo reads the passes like they're printed in a playbook. She intercepts two in a row, and the Year Sixes on the sideline start chanting her name.

'JO! JO! JO!'

Ava shines. She feeds perfect passes into the ring and keeps the pressure on. Even when East Ridge gets ***physical***, she doesn't flinch.

Cassandra sinks another goal.

Then another.

6–3 to Talma Valley.

But East Ridge equalises and then pull into the lead.

The score is 5–6 at three-quarter-time.

Jo's glugging down water and jamming an orange quarter into her mouth.

Everyone's trying to catch their breath. Then, Max calls out from the sidelines, 'Time to go full beast mode, Talma Valley!'

As if on cue, Billie barks. The whole team hears. They're ready to give it everything they've got.

Jo shadows her Goal Attack, sticks tight to her, and when the ball swings wide into the goal third, she's already there.

One step. Two.

Jo grabs it, fumbles slightly but regains her footing and fires it to Jane at Centre.

Jane swings it to Ava.

Ava loops it to Cassandra at the edge of the circle.

She shoots.

Goal.

6–6.

There's twenty seconds left on the clock. East Ridge rushes the centre pass.

The ball goes back into play, but Jo's alert and she sees her moment.

She tips it and there's a loose ball. Ava gets there first. She ***scoops*** it, dodges her player and finds Jane.

Jane to Tamsin.

Tamsin to Cassandra, now deep in the shooting third.

Just seconds left.

Cassandra steadies.

Shoots.

The ball drops – clean through the hoop.

The siren blares.

7–6. Talma Valley wins.

The court explodes. Everyone is cheering and hugging.

Coach Miriam pumps both fists in the air. Mr Redfern claps ***proudly***. But the loudest cheer comes from Mrs Jensen.

Jo turns to Ava, who's still catching her breath.

'We did it,' Ava says. 'We won the championship!'

Jo can hardly believe it, but it's true. 'We did. We really did!'

CHAPTER TWENTY

The Monday at school after the grand final feels especially quiet.

There are still high-fives in the corridor and a giant 'CONGRATS NETBALL CHAMPS' banner in the library, but the storm of excitement has passed. It's back-to-school business as usual and that weird smell from the Science wing.

The classroom intercom crackles to life. 'Jo Weston and Ava Harris to the office, please. Jo Weston and Ava Harris.'

The class turns as Jo and Ava exchange a ***puzzled*** look. Their teacher nods them off, and they slip out of their seats.

'You think it's about the game?' Ava whispers as they exit the classroom.

'Maybe,' Jo says. 'We're not in trouble, are we?'

They reach the front office, where Mrs Bell waits just inside the door, her usual calm expression touched with a hint of mischief.

'In here, girls.' She ushers them inside the office.

A cardboard box sits open on the table beside a stack of assembly programs. Tissue paper spills over the sides.

'I was sorting the end-of-term awards,' she says, 'and look what I found.'

She peels back the tissue.

There it is: the original netball trophy. It's ***unmistakable*** with its dented side.

Ava gasps. 'No way.'

Jo steps closer. 'You're kidding.'

Mrs Bell shakes her head, smiling. 'I don't want to cast blame, but I suspect Alannah accidentally packed up the wrong set of trophies, poor dear. I had asked her to get the awards trophies ready and she also did some dusting for me in the cabinet. A simple mistake.'

'So, no one took it,' Jo says slowly. 'It just got . . .'

'Misplaced,' Mrs Bell says gently. 'And Alannah's finished up now, so I'd rather she doesn't know she was the cause of so much ***angst***. And I'd like Mr Redfern to give her a good report for her work experience. She really was very helpful.'

Jo nods slowly. 'Of course. Your secret's safe with us.'

Mrs Bell picks up the trophy and holds it out to Jo. 'But now we've got two trophies.'

Jo stares down at the trophy. It feels strange seeing it now, after everything they've been through.

'I thought maybe you'd know what to do with it,' says Mrs Bell.

Jo knows ***immediately*** where this trophy belongs. 'I do.'

CHAPTER TWENTY-ONE

Ava and Jo hover outside Mrs Jensen's office.

'What if she turns up?' whispers Jo.

'She'll be with the Year Fours for another few minutes.' Ava holds the office door open for Jo.

Jo nods. 'You cover me.'

She slips through the door and closes it softly behind her.

The office is quiet. Tidy, as always. The smell of peppermint tea lingers faintly in the air. Jo crosses to the desk and places the original netball trophy squarely in the centre.

She grabs a sticky note from the pad beside the keyboard, uncaps a pen and writes quickly.

This one belongs to you.

– From the team.

It feels right to give Mrs Jensen the trophy that she helped the team win last year. And for her to know what her **commitment** to the team meant.

Jo sticks it to the base of the trophy, then pauses. On the desk, propped in its little wooden stand, today's motivational quote catches her eye.

Focus on the work. Let others worry about the spotlight.

Jo smiles.

Then she's gone, the door clicking shut behind her.

CHAPTER TWENTY-TWO

'I still can't believe the trophy was found,' says Jo.

'Make that two,' says Ava.

Jo, Ava, Jane and Tamsin wait outside The Milk Bar. Billie sits beside them, tail ***thudding*** steadily against the pavement.

'I'm just glad Cassandra and Max are friends again,' Jo adds.

'They might not be after Max finds out what she did to the basketball team,' Jane says with a grin.

'Ooh yes! Their final is next week,' says Tamsin.

They all laugh. Billie barks once, like she's in on the joke.

Cassandra and Max appear around the corner, with Kiki and Rose not far behind.

'You're early,' says Cassandra. 'We thought maybe you'd been pulled into another ***investigation***.'

'No missing persons,' says Jo. 'Unless you count Billie, who tried to chase a magpie and nearly fell into a wheelie bin.'

'She's a menace,' says Max, stepping back just as Billie wags her tail ***enthusiastically*** at him.

'She's a little *nutty*,' Jo agrees, scratching Billie behind the ears.

Billie barks again and drops a crumpled leaf at Jo's feet like it's fresh evidence.

'I think that's her way of saying it's puppychino time,' says Cassandra.

They file into The Milk Bar. Larry waves from behind the counter as they split across two booths. Billie settles by the door, happily licking frothy milk from a paper cup.

Jo leans back in her seat, watching her friends talk, laugh, interrupt each other. She wraps her hands around a chocolate milkshake and lets the moment sink in. Then a thought strikes her.

This ***mystery*** might be over. But she knows there will be more.

ABOUT JO WESTON

Jo Weston grew up on her parents' nut farm in rural Victoria. She moved to Melbourne at age six and soon after joined the Waverley Netball Club, where her love of netball began. Jo is now a senior member of both the Melbourne Vixens and Australian Diamonds.

As one of Australia's best defenders, Jo helped lead the Diamonds to gold at the 2022 Commonwealth Games and the 2023 World Cup. With the Melbourne Vixens Jo was instrumental in the team's Premiership win in 2020 and Minor Premiership of 2022.

Away from the court, Jo is passionate about environmental causes, her beloved Essendon FC and her Australian Shepherd, Billie.